Art Editor Toni Rann
Senior Editor Jane Yorke
Photography Stephen Oliver
Series Consultant Neil Morris
Editorial Director Sue Unstead
Art Director Anne-Marie Bulat

This is a Dorling Kindersley Book
published by Random House, Inc.

First American edition, 1990

Library of Congress Cataloging-in-Publication Data
My first look at sizes.
    p.   cm.
    Summary: Photographs explore the concept of size,
including big and little, big, bigger, biggest, and same size.
    ISBN 0-679-80532-X
    1. Size perception - Juvenile literature. [1. Size.] I. Title: Sizes.
BF299.S5M9   1990
152.14 - dc20   89-63086   CIP AC

Manufactured in Italy   4 5 6 7 8 9 0

Phototypeset by Windsorgraphics, Ringwood, Hampshire
Reproduced in Hong Kong by Bright Arts
Printed in Italy by L.E.G.O.

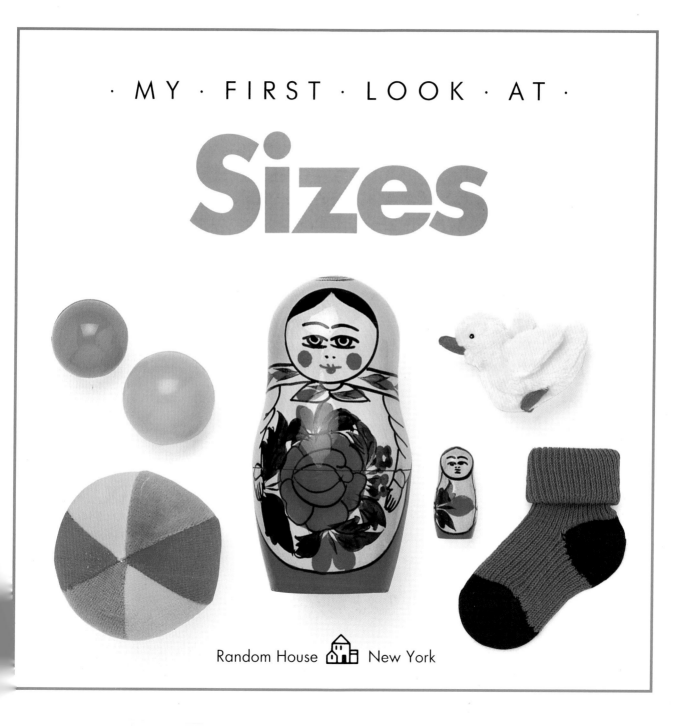

· MY · FIRST · LOOK · AT ·

Sizes

Random House New York

Big

mug

glove

clown

duck

train

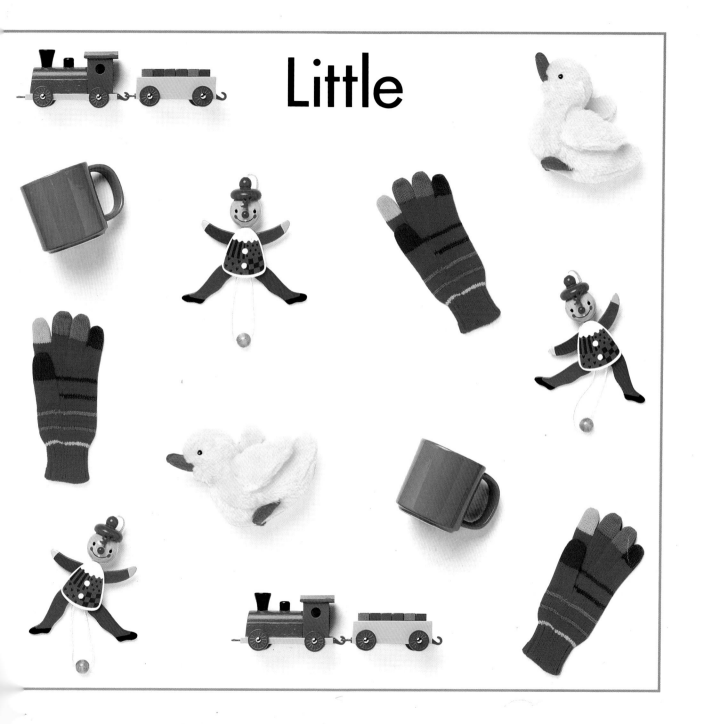

Little

Little to big

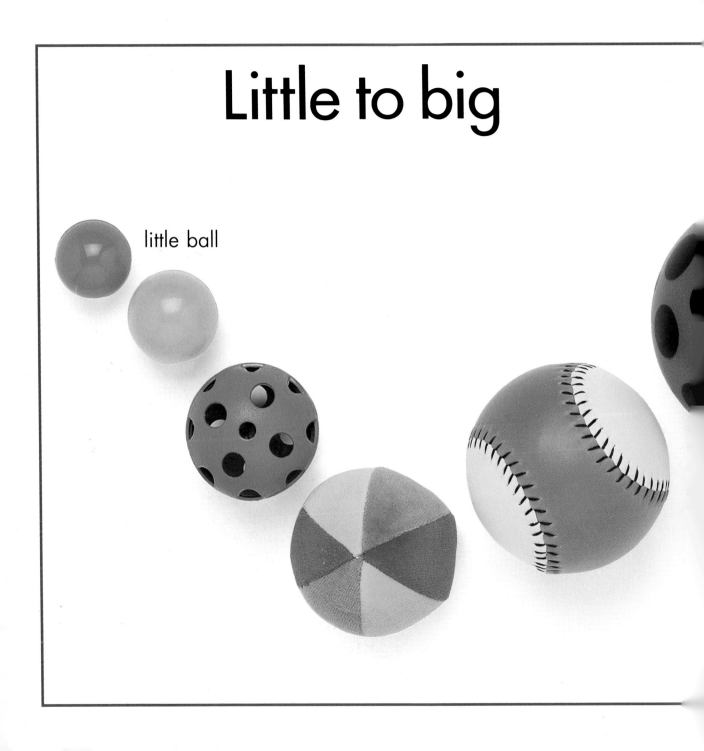

little ball

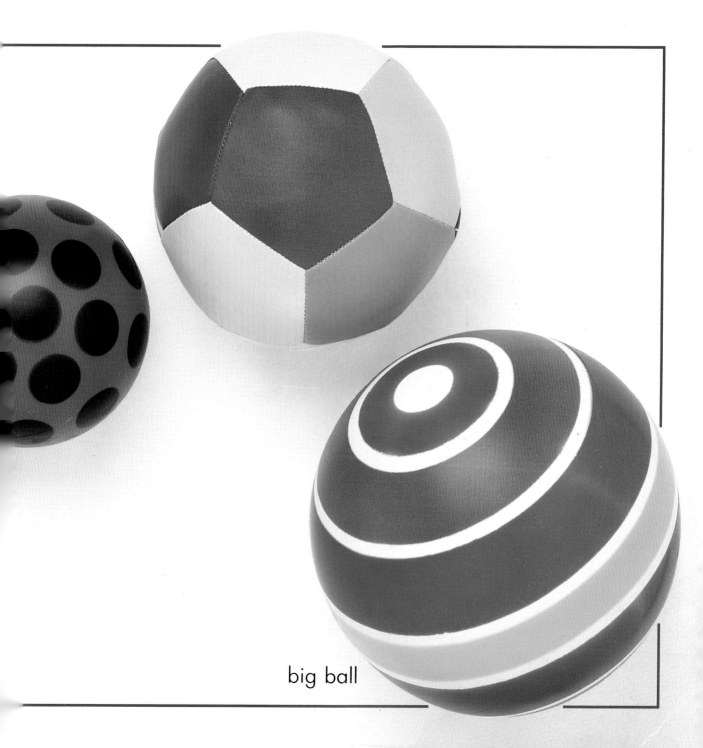

big ball

Big to little

big shell

little
shell

Big, bigger, biggest

big present

bigger present

biggest present

small doll

smaller doll

Small, smaller, smallest

smallest
doll

Which is the smallest cup?

Tiny things

Same size

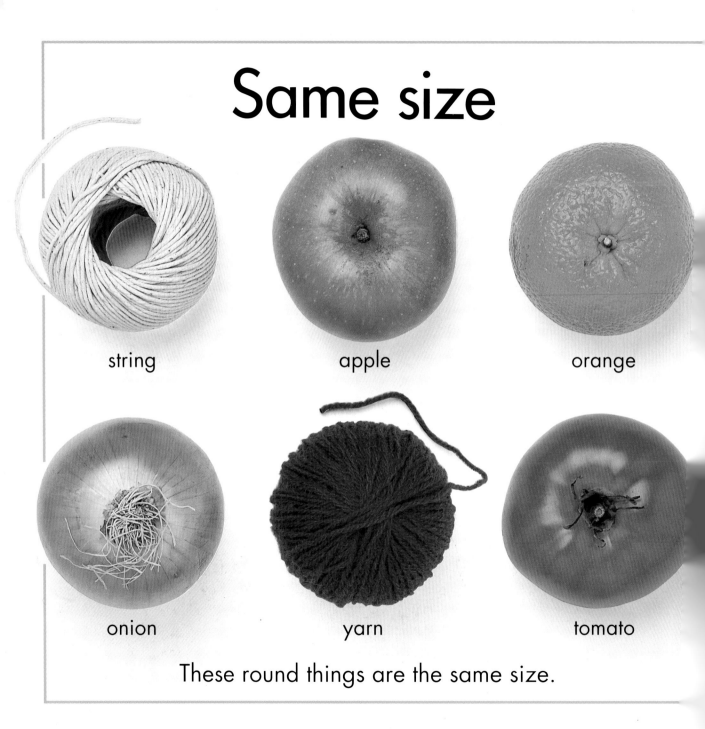

string

apple

orange

onion

yarn

tomato

These round things are the same size.

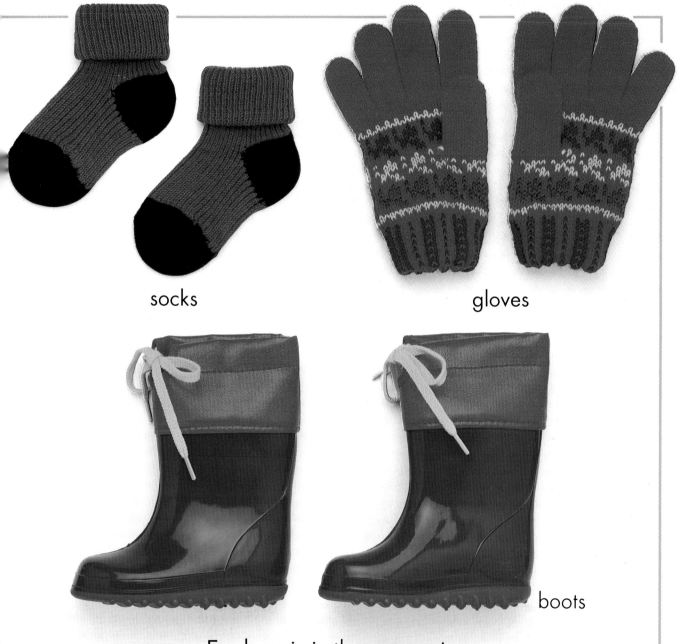

socks

gloves

boots

Each pair is the same size.

Growing

Our hands get bigger as we grow.

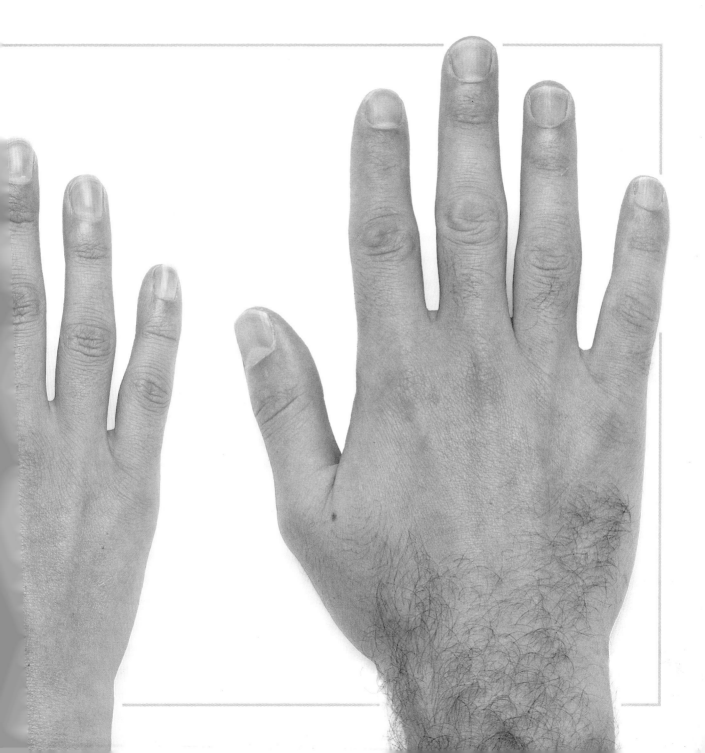